Hello Kitty

and friends

The Camping Trip

·A HELLO KITTY ADVENTURE·

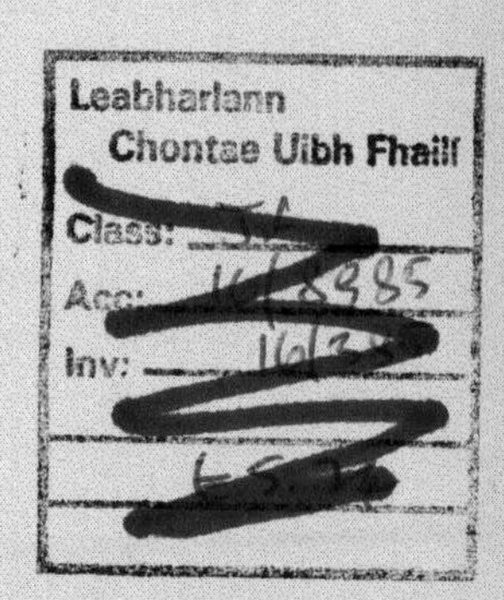

The Camping Trip

•A HELLO KITTY ADVENTURE•

HarperCollins *Children's Books*

MEET
Hello Kitty
and friends
Mimmy
Hello Kitty
Tammy

Mama
Papa
Grandpa
Grandma
Fifi
Dear Daniel

With special thanks to
Linda Chapman and Michelle Misra

First published in Great Britain by HarperCollins Children's Books in 2015

www.harpercollins.co.uk
1 3 5 7 9 10 8 6 4 2

ISBN: 978-0-00-754071-6

Printed and bound in England

Contents

Hello Kitty stood back from her bed and looked at her packing – her clothes were in neat rows, her hair bows were set out, her shoes were in a line and her pink flowery sleeping bag was all rolled up. She hadn't forgotten anything, had she? Just then, her twin sister Mimmy bounced into the room with a backpack. Mimmy **laughed** and pointed out that Hello Kitty might have put out all of the things that she *wanted* to take camping but hadn't she forgotten the most important things?

What sort of things? Hello Kitty looked at everything she had laid out.

Mimmy started pulling things out of her backpack and putting them on the bed next to

Hello Kitty's things. She had:

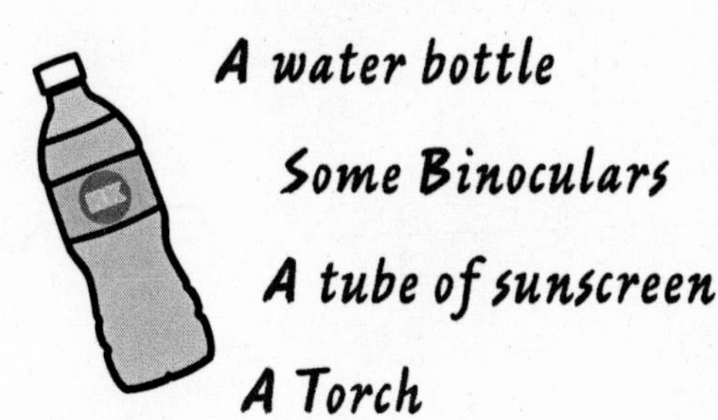

A water bottle

Some Binoculars

A tube of sunscreen

A Torch

Hello Kitty grinned. Mimmy was right! They did need to take things like that, but she was having lots of fun packing things to wear. After all, she wanted to look nice when they got there!

At that moment,

Mama White came in and gasped when she saw what Hello Kitty was planning on taking. They were going away for a weekend, not a whole month! She smiled and said that Hello Kitty would need to put some of it back – or there wouldn't be any room in the tent for the Friendship Club!

Hello Kitty *giggled* and thought about her friends in the Friendship Club – Dear Daniel, Fifi and Tammy. Usually the four of them met after school and in the holidays to do all sorts of fun things like arts and crafts, baking and having sleepovers, but this weekend Hello Kitty's parents were taking them camping. Mama and Papa were going to be in one tent and Hello Kitty and the Friendship Club would be in the

one next door, as well as Mimmy and her friend Alice. It was going to be so much *fun!*

Hello Kitty looked back at her things. Perhaps some of the clothes she'd put out could go back in the wardrobe. But wasn't there a barbecue night during the weekend? If there was, she'd need a special outfit for that. Hello Kitty picked up the brochure for where they were going – Camp Funday – and started flicking through the pages.

Excitement *fizzed* through her as she looked at all of the photos and read about the camp activities. Camp Funday was deep in a forest and had lots of exciting things to do – not just camping, but swimming, climbing and hiking as well. There was an adventure playground and a small farm with rabbits and goats and small animals that could be cuddled. But the main attractions were the nature trails that ran through the forest! Papa White had hired a big camper van to get them all there.

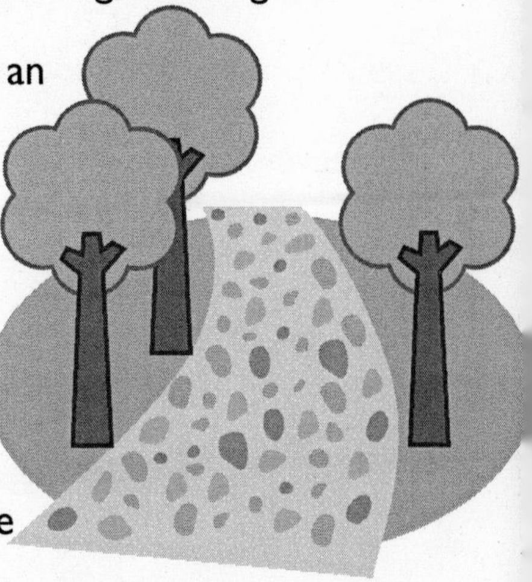

Hello Kitty started imagining what it would be like with a whole forest to play in with her friends. She was lost in thought when suddenly, she heard a *crash* from outside! She ran over to her window and looked out. Papa White was lying in the garden with his feet in the air and a folded-up tent covering him.

He must have been practising putting it up – but he clearly wasn't doing it right!

Hello Kitty tried not to giggle as she ran down the stairs with Mimmy to help Papa up. He thanked both the girls and then shook his head as he looked at the tent lying flat on the ground in front of him. This was harder than he had remembered!

Hello Kitty and Mimmy helped him to stand the tent back up, and then Papa White went all round it, pegging down the ropes that held it in place. He hammered the pegs with a little mallet… one… two… three… four… Finally, he stood back proudly to admire the now set-up tent in front of him. Until… *whoosh*… it collapsed on the grass again. Hello Kitty and Mimmy giggled.

Oh **bother!** Papa White was quite red in the face now. It was hot outside in the summer sun and putting up the tent was thirsty work. He grumbled; maybe going camping wasn't such a good idea after all! But then he **grinned** at the girls. He'd figure it out in the end!

At that moment, Mama White appeared. She smiled at Papa, and wondered aloud if maybe a break of home-made lemonade and some chocolate biscuits might help him feel better... Then he could have another look at the tent.

They all agreed that it was a good plan.

As they stood in the sunshine drinking their cool drinks, Hello Kitty thought about all the fun they were going to have at Camp Funday – toasting marshmallows on the campfire, telling stories and tucked up under the stars in their tents. She was so excited – she didn't know how she would ever get to sleep that night!

The next day, Hello Kitty and Mimmy were up bright and early. They were packed and ready by the door when Dear Daniel, Tammy and Fifi arrived. Alice was dropped off soon after and in no time at all, the friends were standing together in the driveway, ***chattering*** excitedly. All that was left was to pack up the camper van and head off!

Dear Daniel squeezed into the back row of seats with Tammy and Alice beside him, and Hello Kitty sat with Fifi and Mimmy in the next row. Mama White was in the front seat, while Papa White climbed in the driver's side and took the wheel. That was it – they were **off!**

They **sped** past shops and houses until the view changed into open fields as they left the sights and sounds of the city far behind them.

Papa White looked back at everyone in the mirror and suggested that they should try singing some camping songs! Soon they were all singing along as **loudly** as they could...

Ten green bottles, hanging on the wall…

Ten green bottles, hanging on the wall…

And if one green bottle should accidentally fall,

There'll be NINE green bottles, hanging on the wall…!

Hello Kitty and her friends sang at the top of their voices, **laughing**, and Mama White put her hands over her ears. Luckily she didn't have to listen to them for long as just then, they turned into a long tree-lined driveway with a sign that read CAMP FUNDAY. They were here!

Papa White pulled up at a wooden gate where an attendant checked their booking and then pointed them down a track to the left that led deep into the heart of the forest. Soon they were parking in a shady glade, where colourful tents were already pitched around them.

KT I

Hello Kitty and her friends jumped out. *Wow!* A big canopy of trees stood overhead and the smell of pine needles filled the air. Everyone wanted to go and explore, but Mama White said that they had to put their tents up first, and have some lunch as well.

Papa looked around. It would be good to pitch their tents somewhere quiet, and it would need to be a spot that was completely flat as well.

Tammy pointed out a shady spot under the trees where the floor was covered in lovely soft pine

needles, so it would be nice and soft for them to sleep on too.

It looked just perfect! Papa White went to get the tents from the camper van while everyone else started to clear any stones or twigs from the ground, to make sleeping a lot more comfortable.

They all set to work. Soon, the area for the tents was completely clear. Dear Daniel laid out the two ground sheets and Papa White put both of the tents on top – a green one and a blue one. Hello Kitty and the rest of the Friendship Club **smoothed** them out till there weren't

any creases or folds in them, and then started threading in the tent poles that would hold them up. Finally, Papa went round the outside of the first tent, pulling the ropes taut and hammering the pegs into the ground.

Hooray! Everyone let out a loud cheer when the first tent – the green one – went up. It was for two people, so perfect for Mama and Papa to sleep in. Papa smiled. That hadn't been so bad!

Practising the day before HAD helped after all. Now it was time for the really big blue tent that the rest of them were going to sleep in. Papa went around the outside of the tent, pulling on the ropes and hammering in the pegs. A group of children from some nearby tents gathered to watch.

As Papa White set up the tent, everything was going well. He hammered in all the pegs and pulled on the ropes again, until he got to the final rope – and the tent popped up into the air! The children who were watching burst out laughing. **Oh no!** Papa hadn't quite got it right this time.

Some of the poles hadn't been in properly so what was meant to be a sturdy, tunnel-shaped tent had a big floppy bit in the middle.

Papa White sighed and started again. Hello Kitty looked at the laughing children watching and **sighed** too. She thought it was mean of them to laugh. But soon all of the poles were secured back in place and the little tent pegs were hammered into the ground.

Ta da! The blue tent went up perfectly this time! Papa smiled and nodded at her as Hello Kitty ran over to the door and unzipped it to look inside. She called to her friends, and they all took off their shoes and stepped inside.

Hello Kitty glanced over at the other children before she followed her friends. They looked like they were about to come and say hello… but then they were called away to lunch. Hello Kitty was **glad** – she wasn't sure they seemed very nice anyway.

The Friendship Club were all very excited as they went into the tent. All that was left to do was for Hello Kitty to add the finishing touches – some flowery bunting that she had brought with her to make the inside of the tent look extra pretty!

There was just enough time for them to spread out their sleeping bags and unpack their things before lunch. Mama had brought a lovely big picnic and was setting it up outside.

Hello Kitty smoothed out her sleeping bag and put her nightdress on her pillow. It had a big red strawberry on the front.

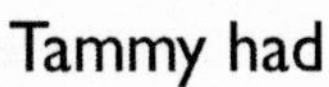

Tammy had brought along a book and a pencil case, Fifi had brought along her toy rabbit, and Dear Daniel had brought along a torch and a small round metal thing. What was it? Hello Kitty picked it up to take a look, and Dear Daniel explained that it was a compass and that all good adventurers had one. He pointed out the points of the compass – north, south, east and west, and showed her how the little arrow *flickered* and showed them which direction they were going in. **Look!** They were pointing south right now.

Hello Kitty thought it looked really interesting! But there wasn't time to look at it any more just then – lunch was ready!

Hello Kitty stuck her head out of the tent and saw that Mama had spread out a red and white checked cloth on the grass. Suddenly she realised how hungry she was! Soon everyone was munching their way through sandwiches, carrot and cucumber sticks and cool glasses of juice. **Yum!** They all agreed that food always tasted twice as good outdoors!

3 Exploring the Trails

When lunch was over, Mama packed the picnic things away and suggested that the girls and their friends spend the afternoon exploring. They could look all over the camp but they weren't to go out on the trails – they should save those until tomorrow, when they would have a full day to explore. In the meantime, Mama and Papa were going to relax and read their books in the afternoon sun.

Hello Kitty couldn't wait to head off. Camp Funday was completely fenced in and there were people **everywhere** – walking their dogs, playing and generally having fun – so she knew that they would be safe!

Mimmy and Alice wanted to go and look at the little farm first, while Hello Kitty, Tammy, Fifi and Dear Daniel decided to take a look at the entrance to the trails, then go to the adventure playground.

The two groups waved goodbye to each other and headed out from the glade. Just as they were passing through the trees, Fifi saw a little ***flash***

of colour in the bracken – a bob of brown and white that flashed past her. She quickly pointed it out to the others. A deer! They knew that the camp had deer in the forest but hadn't thought they would be lucky enough to see one so quickly! **Super!**

Soon they reached a big noticeboard with a map on it that showed the trails. There were four; the yellow trail – which was the easiest –

led through the meadow, and around the lake and back; the green one went past the barbecue area and back; the blue went through the beginning of the forest and over a stream, and the red one – the **hardest** – took them into the heart of the woods. All the trails were marked out with colourful arrows and they all came back to the same starting point. Hello Kitty, Dear Daniel, Tammy and Fifi decided to go and look at the start of the yellow trail. They had told Mama they wouldn't go exploring yet but there was no harm in having a look!

When they got to the start of the yellow trail they found the children who had been watching them put up their tents that morning – there were two girls about the same age as the Friendship Club and two younger boys. The boys were fighting with sticks and the two girls were pulling branches across the start of the yellow trail.

When the girls saw Hello Kitty, Dear Daniel, Tammy and Fifi they **smiled** and asked them if they wanted to play with them.

Hmmm. Hello Kitty wasn't sure she did; she hadn't liked it when they had laughed at Papa that morning and the way the boys were fighting with sticks looked **dangerous!**

But Fifi smiled and asked what the girls were doing. They grinned back. They thought the yellow trail was too easy, and

they were trying to make the trail more difficult!

Hello Kitty shook her head quickly. She didn't think they should be doing that. If the girls pulled branches across the trail then people pushing babies in buggies ***wouldn't*** be able to get past. One of the girls stuck her tongue out. Hello Kitty wasn't very happy about that, but she stayed calm and pointed out that she was just being sensible.

The trail was for *everyone!* The girl looked thoughtful for a second, but then she just shrugged.

The other girl, who had curly dark hair, stepped forward and smiled shyly. Why didn't they all go and do something more exciting – did Hello Kitty and the others want to explore some of the harder trails with them? It could be **fun** if they all went together.

Hello Kitty said thank you, but they couldn't – they had

to get back to Hello Kitty's parents. The girl who had stuck out her tongue looked at her and made *clucking* noises like a chicken, and then she and the others ran off **giggling!**

Hello Kitty gasped. She thought that was very rude of them…

Dear Daniel smiled at Hello Kitty. It was fine. They had just been playing!

Hello Kitty announced that even if they had just been playing, it was silly for them to put branches across the start of the trail. The rest of the Friendship Club agreed. They pulled the branches away from the path so that people could still use the trail. **There**... all fixed.

They turned around and went to explore the rest of the campsite. Hello Kitty still felt a bit funny about the way the other children had acted, so Dear Daniel tried to cheer her up.

Look! He pointed high in the sky to where the sun was *streaming* through the trees, making colourful patterns on the trails.

Hello Kitty smiled. It was very pretty. But Dear Daniel shook his head. It was important to know which direction you were going in when you were walking, and the sun showed them that. He pointed out that if they went down the trails they'd be walking directly into the sun, which meant that they'd be walking west!

Fifi gave a skip. She thought that was very interesting, but why would they need to know from the sun? They had a compass after all – that would tell them which direction they were going!

Dear Daniel grinned and threw out his hands. He'd been trying to *cheer* Hello Kitty up, and maybe they would need to know one day!

But for now they should just go off to explore the park. Fifi and Tammy shouted yes, and Hello Kitty grinned back and joined in. **Hooray!**

They ran to the adventure playground and soon they were playing on zip wires, sliding down slides and swinging on tyres.

After a long while it was time to head back to the tents for dinner. Papa was just lighting a campfire when they walked into the glade, and Mimmy and Alice were sitting on a log watching him and **waiting** for their dinner.

After a delicious dinner cooked on the open fire, with toasted marshmallows to finish, Hello Kitty and her friends sang under the light of the night stars. It was just starting to get dark as Hello Kitty started yawning. She couldn't wait to snuggle down in her sleeping bag – it had been a long day. A long but very fun day. And who knew what adventures lay ahead of them tomorrow!

4 Following the Path

When Hello Kitty woke up the next morning, she couldn't remember where she was. Then when she felt the sun ***streaming*** through the gap in the tent and saw her friends in sleeping bags around her, it all came back and she smiled.

Quickly she called to the others to get up. They had the whole day ahead of them and they didn't want to waste it! Mama and Papa were already up when Hello Kitty unzipped the front of the tent and stepped outside. Hello Kitty was *surprised* that Mama hadn't woken them up, but Mama said that she had wanted to let them sleep.

It had been a long day yesterday and an even longer night – she had heard them all talking after lights out AND using their torches… But Mama White wasn't annoyed. That was what camping was all about!

After breakfast Hello Kitty was **excited** to get going but before they went, Mama made sure that their water bottles were filled and that they had plenty of snacks in their backpacks. They

were going to be on the trails for the whole day, after all, and serious adventurers needed serious food supplies!

Alice and Mimmy wanted to set off on their own again, so Hello Kitty and her friends packed everything up for their own day. Soon they were all **ready** and trekking across Camp Funday to the start of the trails.

Tammy thought they should do the trails in order, and so they started with the yellow one. It was very easy but it would take them **through** the meadow and around the lake, so they would see lots of ducks and geese. The morning sun was just starting to break through the clouds as they walked around the water and pointed out

the birds to each other. Boats **bobbed** on the water as they came back to the start, and on to the green trail. They walked past the BBQ area and then back again. It was easy to see where they were going as green arrows were attached to trees, or on posts to mark the way clearly.

It was quiet and peaceful as they headed into the woods on the blue trail. And just as well as it was starting to get quite hot, with the sun high in the sky now. Just as they were turning into the trees, Hello Kitty heard a noise behind them.

She turned round and saw the four children from yesterday. ***Hmmm.*** The girl who had stuck out her tongue came over and said hello, and introduced herself as Rebecca. She announced loudly that she had seen that they were doing the trails – were they going to try the red trail next? Hello Kitty said that they were and Rebecca **giggled** and went back to her friends. They all smiled together as they walked off, and called out to the Friendship Club to have a good walk.

Hello Kitty said that they would and started walking into the woods with her friends following. Once they finished the blue trail, they started on the red.

Straightaway they all realised that the red trail was much more **difficult!** The path was rough and they often had to push their way through bushes and climb over logs. The arrows were spaced out so far that at times they felt nervous that they weren't even on the right trail!

After a while Dear Daniel suggested they put down some patterans – things that proper explorers used to mark their routes that his Dad had told him about. You

put down sticks or leaves in special ways to show the way you had been walking – in case you needed to get back and forgot which path you had been walking on. They were very useful when the path forked in two. **Look!**

He found three sticks and then carefully placed them on the ground at a fork in the trail, with one stick pointing in the direction they were going and the other two at the head of it, to look like an arrow. The girls thought it was really **clever!** When Dear Daniel was finished they all stepped over the sticks to follow the red signposts, which pointed over a stile and towards a gate.

Dear Daniel stayed a bit behind and carefully put down a leaf and two stones as well, and

Fifi called back to him to catch up. Dear Daniel **smiled** at her and called back that she should be patient! They weren't in a rush after all. When he caught up, they all climbed over the stile and went through the gate. They looked around – where were the arrows to show them where to go? Hmmm. They couldn't find any so they followed the path; they were sure they would

find some arrows soon. But although they walked and walked, they didn't see any.

Dear Daniel *kept* stopping every so often to put down leaves and sticks as patterans. It was interesting at first, but it DID keep slowing them down. Even Tammy was starting to *hop* from foot to foot while they waited for Dear Daniel.

Finally, they reached a waterfall. They'd been walking for what felt like *forever!* Mountains of water splashed down, throwing up a spray all around them and a cold mist filled the air. It looked beautiful, but there didn't seem to be any way round it, and they couldn't see any red arrows *anywhere!*

This was strange. Where were they supposed to go now?

Dear Daniel scratched his head as they all looked around. They could try climbing the rocks and going round the waterfall that way, but Fifi didn't like that idea. They should look really hard for an arrow instead. There must be one

somewhere!

Tammy suggested that they split up to look for one, but Hello Kitty didn't think that was a very good idea. They should definitely stick together. They searched and searched but try as they might, they couldn't find a red arrow.

In the end Hello Kitty took a deep breath and declared that they should go back to the start of the trail. They'd just have to go back the way they came.

But which was the way back?

Oh no! They'd been so busy searching for the arrows that they didn't know where they were. They were **lost!**

Dear Daniel gave a small smile. Not to worry. He had his compass in his pocket, so they just needed to check which way was east and then they could head that way to get back to the camp. He reached into his pocket – but it was completely ***empty!*** The compass was ***gone!*** It must have fallen out of his pocket while they were walking. Now what were they going to do? He looked at the others.

Hello Kitty started to feel a little worried. It was getting a bit colder and the afternoon sun had started to disappear. Tammy looked like she might cry. If they didn't get back soon, they might be trapped in the woods all night!

Dear Daniel told them that they should all keep **calm**. He reminded them that the sun out on the trails was from the west when they saw it yesterday, so they would just need to walk away from the sun, to the east, to get home.

Hello Kitty felt a wave of relief. He was ***right!*** And so they started back, walking away from the sun. They found what looked like it might be a trail, and suddenly, Tammy pointed to something on the ground.

It was a patteran – Dear Daniel's last one – of a leaf and two stones. They walked on a little further. Look! There was another. They were definitely on the right **track!** The trail led them back to the gate and on to the path. Now they were able to run through the woods, following the red arrows all the way back. They ran faster and faster and before they knew it, they were back at the start of the trails. **Phew!** They were all very happy to be out of the woods.

Hello Kitty turned to Dear Daniel and the others. They should get back to the tents so that Mama and Papa didn't worry; they were already much later than they had said they would be.

They ***raced*** back towards the tents, but just as they came near Tammy pointed ahead and Mama and Papa White came rushing towards them. They had been just about to organise a search party!

Hello Kitty explained what had happened – how they had been doing just fine on the trail – until they had reached the waterfall and couldn't see any more arrows to tell them which way to go.

Dear Daniel joined in and said that they had lost their compass as well, so they had to follow the sun to get back to the trail, and then they had used his patterans to guide them. He explained about putting down sticks and leaves so they could see where they'd been.

Mama and Papa White couldn't believe it when they heard the story. Thank goodness that Dear Daniel had known what to do! But what could have happened to the arrows marking the trail?

Papa was sure they shouldn't have led to a waterfall. That didn't sound right at all.

Just then, a voice called

out from behind them. It was the girl they had met before – Rebecca. She was racing towards them, followed by her parents and the other girl and boys. They all looked very *worried!* Rebecca stammered that she hadn't meant for anything bad to happen and asked if the Friendship Club were all OK.

Hello Kitty was confused. How had Rebecca known that she and the others had been lost? Rebecca's parents looked **very** unhappy. They explained that Rebecca had told them that she and her friends had changed the way the arrow by the gate pointed, so that it led towards the waterfall instead of pointing the right way!

Rebecca started to **sniffle.** It had just been a joke, she whispered – she hadn't meant for Hello Kitty and her friends to get into trouble. They had just wanted them to get a little bit lost – she had wanted to play a trick because she was upset that they hadn't wanted to be friends. She had known they had a compass and thought that they would be fine, but then she and the others had found the compass out on the trail where Dear Daniel must have dropped it.

She had been really worried then so had run to tell her parents – they had been coming to sound the alarm just then! Rebecca held out the compass to Dear Daniel. She was so sorry. The other children hung their heads and said sorry too. They wouldn't be able to go to the barbecue that night as a punishment.

Mama looked at Papa, and then Hello Kitty spoke up.

No harm had been done and everything was OK. Rebecca had said she was sorry and she had done the right thing in owning up; that was very brave of her. And Hello Kitty said quietly that maybe SHE could have been nicer, and given the others a chance to be friends.

They all looked at each other. Mama White pointed out that the barbecue was about to start and that would give everyone the perfect chance to get to know each other properly, wouldn't it? They all looked at each other and smiled shyly, as Rebecca and Hello Kitty nodded.

Hooray!

Hello Kitty and her friends sat ***happily*** around the campfire, munching on their dinner. They were eating delicious hamburgers and sausages in soft, squidgy buns with lots of sauce. The barbecue area had been decorated with little fairy lights that hung from the trees, lighting up the night sky and making the area look **really** pretty.

Hello Kitty looked around the fire at everyone chattering happily – friends both old and new – and felt a warm **glow** spread through her tummy. It was so much fun being part of a big group!

Rebecca and the others had turned out to be very nice and really good fun after all. They'd just got off on the wrong foot with each other.

When they had all finished eating, Hello Kitty suggested that they all play a game together.

They all thought hard – **Oooh!** What about sardines? The perfect camping game! Hello Kitty would hide first.

Hello Kitty headed off as everyone counted down behind her. Five, four, three, two, one... She found a spot, right behind a big mossy log. Vines and branches that had dropped down hid it. She thought that they would never find her but in no time at all, she was joined by Dear Daniel.

Hello Kitty gave her friend a **big** hug. Thank goodness he had known about the sun and the patterans. It could have gotten them in a whole load of trouble if they hadn't followed them back!

Dear Daniel agreed, but there was something more important than that – something that he thought should become a Friendship Club saying. Especially since they were playing this game...

Hello Kitty looked *puzzled*. What was it? Dear Daniel explained that everything would have been fine if they had become friends with the other children in the first place. So the new saying should be:

He thought that would make a very good Friendship Club motto indeed – especially since… he gave a shout as Rebecca **jumped** over the log and **squeezed** in beside them, **giggling.**

Hello Kitty grinned and agreed.

But there wasn't any time to tell Rebecca – as... **BOO!** Everyone else found them and pounced, throwing handfuls of fallen leaves at each other before they all collapsed together in fits of giggles. Hello Kitty **beamed.** Camping trips were the best way of spending a weekend – EVER!

Turn over the page for activities and fun things that you can do with your friends – just like Hello Kitty!

Camping Craziness!

Hello Kitty and her friends had lots of fun on their camping trip, and you can too, even if you can't go away somewhere! Follow the instructions on the following pages to have your own camping fun with dens to build and games to play.

Activity 1

Blanket den

This is one camping trip you can take indoors! You'll need some sheets and blankets, some towels and cushions, and some clothes pegs. Make sure you ask permission from the grown-ups before you move any furniture or take anything out, and get them to help you build!

Hang the blankets and sheets over chairs and furniture to make a hidden, covered space underneath! You can clip any gaps together with clothes pegs, and use towels and cushions to make it cosy inside. It's just like camping outside, inside! Why not make up a password you need to use to get in, or make a name sign for your den?

Activity 2

Scavenger Hunt

Scavenger hunts are lots of fun, and you can play them inside or outside! Each player has a list of small things they need to find, and the first one to collect all the items wins. Look at Hello Kitty's lists below for some ideas of what to collect:

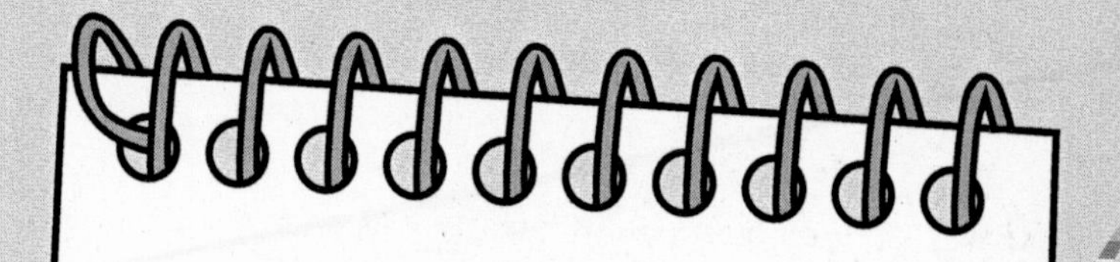

Inside Hunt

- One penny
- A blue button
- A piece of ribbon
- A herb or spice starting with 'C'

Outside Hunt

- A black rock
- A snail shell
- A red leaf
- A forked twig

Activity 3

Story Ring

Telling stories is lots of fun, and telling them with your friends can be even better! In a story ring you all sit together in a circle, and one of you holds a ball. The one holding the ball starts the story off by saying one sentence. They then pass the ball to the next person, who has to continue the story by saying the next sentence! And it keeps going round. Try to keep what you're saying exciting – take a look at some of the Friendship Club's favourite story starters:

Once upon a time, a beautiful princess lived in a castle until the day of her 10th birthday.

All of a sudden Tammy let out a loud scream!

Fifi had never seen anything so big and exciting, so she called out…

Turn the page for a sneak peek at

next adventure...

The Big Bake Off

Hello Kitty stood up and looked down the long row of strawberry plants. She was picking fruit with her twin sister Mimmy and their Mama, at Cherry Tree Farm. It was thirsty work in the hot sun. Mimmy and Hello Kitty's baskets were almost full now, although Hello Kitty thought she had probably eaten as many strawberries as she had picked! Her pink-and-white polka-dot T-shirt was decorated with bright red strawberry stains. Whoops! But she just hadn't been able to resist all the delicious fruit – strawberries, blueberries and raspberries. Yummy!

Hello Kitty sighed happily. What a totally SUPER day they were having. She loved picking fruit and to make the day perfect, her friends were coming over to Hello Kitty's house that afternoon – as soon as she was back from the farm. Hello Kitty felt a warm glow as she thought about Tammy, Fifi and Dear Daniel. Together they made up the Friendship Club. They met after school and in the holidays to do all sorts of fun things – like crafting and painting, having clothes swaps and sleepovers.

Today, however, they were simply meeting up at Hello Kitty's house to play – it was just too hot for much else!

Find out what happens next in...